Ticket to the Moon

An Ivy and Mack story

Contents

Written by Jane Clarke

Illustrated by Gustavo Mazali

with Adrienn Greta Schönberg

Collins

What's in this story?

Listen and say 🎧 1

rainbow

rocket

alien

Chapter 1 We can't wait!

Mack, Ivy, Mum and Dad were at the **airport**.

"I **can't wait** to go on the plane!" said Ivy.

"Me, too!" said Mack. "But Croc wants to go on a rocket."

"I don't think there are any rockets here, Croc," said Ivy.

"Can we get on the plane now, Dad?"
asked Mack.

"Yes, please!" said Ivy.

"Yes, we can. But first we need to wait in a
different line!" said Dad.

They lined up for the machine. When Mack went through it, the machine *bleeped*.

"Have you got something in your **pocket**?" asked the man.

"Yes! My rocket!" Mack told him.

"Sorry," said Dad to the man.

Ivy and Mack watched the planes **take off** and **land**.

"I drew a picture of our plane!" said Ivy.

"*Whoosh!* The rocket takes off!" said Mack.

"Be careful with my coffee!" said Dad.

They waited and waited. Then they went onto the plane and a **flight attendant** showed them where to sit.

"This table goes up and down!" said Mack.

"I'm putting my things behind the seat," said Ivy. "Do you want to get your things out, too, Mack?"

Mack opened his bag. "I can't find Croc!" he said. "Is he in your bag, Ivy?"

Ivy looked in her bag. "He's not here," she said. "Is he in Mum and Dad's bag?"

9

Chapter 2 Croc has a ticket to the moon!

Mum and Dad looked, but they couldn't find Croc.

Mack started to cry. "Croc is **lost**!"

"Oh, Mack," said Mum. "I'm sorry. We know how much you love Croc."

"I want to go home," said Mack.

"Where do you think Croc is?" Mack asked Ivy.

Ivy thought. "*Ummm* ... On a rocket!" she said.

"That's exciting!" said Mack. "He wanted to go on a rocket!"

Ivy looked at Mack. "Let's write Croc's story."

"Yes!" he said.

When the plane took off, Mack and Ivy looked out of the window.

"*Whoosh*!" said Mack. "Croc's rocket takes off! Where's he going, Ivy?"

"Where does he have a ticket to?" said Ivy. "The end of the rainbow?"

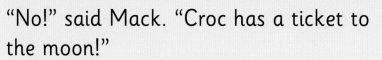

"No!" said Mack. "Croc has a ticket to the moon!"

Ivy took out her paper and pencils. "OK," she said. "That's a good idea, too."

She drew a big rocket.

"Where's the moon?" asked Mack.

"Behind the rainbow," Ivy told him.

"OK," said Mack. "But we need to draw the moon and write some words."

Mack took the paper and a pencil.

Croc has a ticket to the moon!

Chapter 3 On a rocket to the moon

It was time for dinner. The flight attendant came with a **trolley**.

"Would you like pasta or chicken?" he asked.

"Chicken, please," said Ivy.

"Pasta, please," said Mack.

But when the food came, Mack wanted the chicken, so Ivy gave it to him.

"What does Croc eat on his way to the moon?" Mack asked Ivy.

Ivy thought. "Rainbow **drops**!"

"Yes!" said Mack. "And dry fish."

"I don't know how to draw dry fish," said Ivy.

"I do!" said Mack.

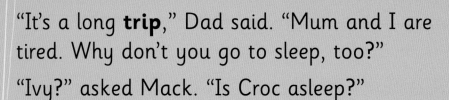

"It's a long **trip**," Dad said. "Mum and I are tired. Why don't you go to sleep, too?"

"Ivy?" asked Mack. "Is Croc asleep?"

"No, he isn't. We can write more of his story," answered Ivy.

"Next, Croc finds a beautiful new star!" said Ivy.

"Yes! It's a **world** full of aliens!" said Mack.

"There aren't any aliens in this story!" said Ivy.

"I want aliens!" answered Mack. "Let's ask Mum and Dad to choose!"

But Mum and Dad were asleep.

"Let's have a star, the moon *and* aliens," said Ivy.

Chapter 4 The first crocodile on the moon!

Ivy and Mack went to sleep. Mack had a dream about Croc and a rocket.

In the morning, Mack and Ivy read *'Ticket to the Moon'* to Mum and Dad.

"Croc finds a new star and goes to the moon!" said Ivy.

"And aliens!" said Mack.

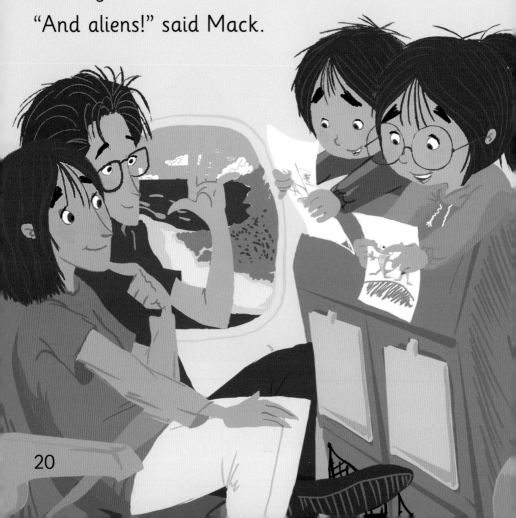

"What an exciting story! What's next?"
asked Mum and Dad.

"Croc looks out of the window of his rocket,"
said Ivy.

"He can see moon rocks!" said Mack.
"Croc's **nearly** there!"

"Croc's rocket lands on the moon!" said Mack. "He goes on a moon walk. He's the first crocodile on the moon!"

Ivy drew a friendly alien in the colours of a rainbow.

"Croc finds a new friend and they live on the moon," she said. "They're very happy. That's a good end to our story, isn't it?"

"No, it isn't!" said Mack.

Chapter 5 Lost and found

Mack looked at Ivy's drawing, "I'm Croc's friend, not that silly alien!"

"But you can't be in the story because you're not on the moon," Ivy told him.

"I want to be with Croc!" Mack started to cry again.

"Can I help?" asked the flight attendant.

"My Croc!" cried Mack. "He went to the moon!"

"Croc is my brother's crocodile," Ivy told him.

"Can the **pilot** help me to find croc?" asked Mack.

"I'm sorry," said the flight attendant. "The pilot doesn't go to the moon."

"I don't like this," said Mack.

"Don't worry," said Ivy. "Croc doesn't need a **passport** on the moon."

"I don't want Croc to be on the moon," said Mack. "I want him here with me."

"We can buy you a new crocodile toy," Mum said.

"That's not the same," said Mack.

"Passports, please!" said the passport man.

They waited for their bags. Their bags came **last**!

Mum looked at Dad. "I was afraid the bags were lost, too!" she said.

Then Mack saw something that made him very happy.

"Croc!" he **shouted**.

Mum and Dad and Ivy all smiled a big smile.

Mack picked up Croc. "Hello, Croc!" he said. "Did you enjoy your trip to the moon?"

Mini-dictionary

Listen and read

airport (noun) An **airport** is a place where people go to fly on an aeroplane.

can't wait (phrase) If you **can't wait** to do something, you really want to do it.

drop (noun) A **drop** is a small round sweet.

flight attendant (noun) A **flight attendant** is a person who works on an aeroplane and looks after the people on it.

land (verb) When an aeroplane **lands**, it comes down to the ground after moving through the air.

last (adverb) Something that comes **last**, comes at the end, or after everything else.

lost (adjective) If something is **lost**, you cannot find it.

nearly (adverb) **Nearly** means the same as almost.

passport (noun) Your **passport** is the important piece of paper that you show when you leave or go into a country.

pilot (noun) The **pilot** is the person who flies an aeroplane.

pocket (noun) A **pocket** in your clothes is a place that you can put things in.

shout (verb) If you **shout**, you say something very loudly.

take off (verb) When an aeroplane **takes off**, it leaves the ground and goes into the air.

trip (noun) A **trip** is when you travel from one place to another.

trolley (noun) A **trolley** is a small table on wheels which sells food and drink.

world (noun) The **world** is the planet we live on.

1 Look and order the story

2 Listen and say

Collins

Published by Collins
An imprint of HarperCollins*Publishers*
Westerhill Road
Bishopbriggs
Glasgow
G64 2QT

HarperCollins*Publishers*
1st Floor, Watermarque Building
Ringsend Road
Dublin 4
Ireland

William Collins' dream of knowledge for all began with the publication of his first book in 1819.

A self-educated mill worker, he not only enriched millions of lives, but also founded a flourishing publishing house. Today, staying true to this spirit, Collins books are packed with inspiration, innovation and practical expertise. They place you at the centre of a world of possibility and give you exactly what you need to explore it.

© HarperCollins*Publishers* Limited 2020

10 9 8 7 6 5 4 3 2

ISBN 978-0-00-839745-6

Collins® and COBUILD® are registered trademarks of HarperCollins*Publishers* Limited

www.collins.co.uk/elt

British Library Cataloguing in Publication Data

A catalogue record for this publication is available from the British Library.

Author: Jane Clarke
Lead illustrator: Gustavo Mazali (Beehive)
Copy illustrator: Adrienn Greta Schönberg (Beehive)
Series editor: Rebecca Adlard
Publishing manager: Lisa Todd
Product managers: Jennifer Hall and Caroline Green
In-house editor: Alma Puts Keren
Project manager: Emily Hooton
Editor: Deborah Friedland
Proofreaders: Natalie Murray and Michael Lamb
Cover designer: Kevin Robbins
Typesetter: 2Hoots Publishing Services Ltd
Audio produced by id audio, London
Reading guide author: Julie Penn
Production controller: Rachel Weaver
Printed and bound by: GPS Group, Slovenia

Download the audio for this book and a reading guide for parents and teachers at www.collins.co.uk/839745